George Murray Humphry

On the Coagulation of the Blood in the Venous System during Life

Anatiposi

George Murray Humphry

On the Coagulation of the Blood in the Venous System during Life

Reprint of the original.

1st Edition 2023 | ISBN: 978-3-38230-452-2

Anatiposi Verlag is an imprint of Outlook Verlagsgesellschaft mbH.

Verlag (Publisher): Outlook Verlag GmbH, Zeilweg 44, 60439 Frankfurt, Deutschland
Vertretungsberechtigt (Authorized to represent): E. Roepke, Zeilweg 44, 60439 Frankfurt, Deutschland
Druck (Print): Books on Demand GmbH, In de Tarpen 42, 22848 Norderstedt, Deutschland

ON THE COAGULATION OF THE BLOOD

IN THE VENOUS SYSTEM DURING LIFE.

ON THE

COAGULATION OF THE BLOOD

IN THE

VENOUS SYSTEM DURING LIFE.

(A THESIS FOR A MEDICAL ACT IN THE UNIVERSITY OF CAMBRIDGE.)

BY

GEORGE MURRAY HUMPHRY, M.D. F.R.S.

SURGEON TO ADDENBROOKE'S HOSPITAL; LECTURER ON ANATOMY IN THE
CAMBRIDGE UNIVERSITY MEDICAL SCHOOL.

(*From the British Medical Journal, with additions.*)

MACMILLAN AND CO.
Cambridge:
AND 23, HENRIETTA STREET, COVENT GARDEN, LONDON.
1859.

COAGULATION OF THE BLOOD.

―――――

I.—CLOTS IN THE VEINS.

THE obstruction of the veins, by clots forming in their interior, has, of late years, been the subject of investigation by several pathologists, who have pointed out clearly the conditions under which it most frequently occurs, and the changes which take place in consequence. Still, doubts appear to exist respecting the causes of the phenomenon, and the starting point of the mischief; and, though the affection is one of very frequent occurrence, and may usually be diagnosed with facility, it certainly has not attracted the attention of practical men so much as it deserves. Very commonly it is suffered to pass unnoticed during life; and, after death, the vessels concerned are seldom examined to a sufficient extent, and with sufficient care, to enable the observer to form a correct opinion upon the matter.

CASE I. My own attention was first particularly directed to this disease, in 1843, by its occurrence in a member of our own profession, a tall, thin, delicate person, who, when just beginning to recover from an attack of pleurisy on the right side, by which he had been much prostrated, experienced an uneasiness and a stiffness in the left groin and side of the

A 2

pelvis. For a day or two he did not pay much attention to the symptom, thinking he had probably strained himself by lying in some awkward position, though there was in reality no ground for such an idea. Soon, however, the uneasiness extended down the thigh into the ham, in the direction of the great vessels, and was accompanied by tenderness in the same part, with swelling on the inner side of the thigh, and enlargement of the superficial veins. It was consequently inferred that there was some affection of the femoral and popliteal veins; and this was rendered quite clear by the extension of the disease to the posterior tibial and lesser saphena veins; the latter of which formed a firm tender cord under the skin. The whole limb also became œdematous. A few leeches were placed over the femoral vein; but it was remarked that very little blood flowed from their bites. Poultices and fomentations were applied to the limb. Gradually the affection subsided, and the limb was restored to its natural condition. When the patient had so far recovered from these attacks as to be able to sit in a chair, he used to wheel himself about the room by means of the right leg, and in this way may have strained the part in some slight degree. At any rate, he began to perceive sensations in the right ham, which excited suspicions of the commencement of an affection there, corresponding with that which had just subsided in the opposite extremity. These suspicions were soon verified by the implication of the lesser saphena vein, and by the gradual extension of the uneasiness and tenderness up the thigh, in the course of the femoral vein, as far as the junction of the saphena major. There was also swelling of the limb. A few leeches were applied; but again very little blood flowed from the bites, in spite of diligent fomentation. The symptoms gradually subsided; and the patient quite recovered. Some œdema of the limbs remained for several months. This entirely disappeared in course of time; the superficial veins resumed their former dimensions; and there was every reason to suppose that the current was re-established through the deep veins. It is worthy of remark that the same patient exhibited symptoms of similar disturbance in the popliteal and femoral veins after each of two subsequent illnesses; viz. after an attack of typhoid fever in 1846, and of pleurisy on the left side in 1851. On the latter occasion, the upper part of the posterior tibial vein and the lesser saphena in the left limb, were involved, as well as the popliteal and femoral. The symptoms were slighter and of shorter duration than in the first attack, and were not followed by any evidences of permanent obstruction to the circulation, or impairment of the limbs.

The following cases occurred soon afterwards.

CASE II. A man, aged 30, not much emaciated, died of phthisis with bronchitis and much prostration. Œdema of the right leg and thigh, with mottled blue and white patches on the skin, like those resulting from ecchymosis, had existed for some days; but had not attracted much attention. The external and internal iliac veins, and part of the common iliac, as well as the femoral, profunda, and saphena major, were distended with coagula, of a dark colour, irregularly intermixed with lighter fibrinous portions, which gave them a mottled aspect. Near the junction of the saphena, the clot was of more uniform colour, presenting the appearance of reddish, soft, dirty lymph, or fibrine, and was adherent to the inner coat of the vein. The latter had lost its polish, was rather soft, and admitted of being peeled off from the outer tunics of the vessel. The cellular tissue immediately surrounding the vein was, especially near the saphena, infiltrated with serum and lymph. The clot terminated abruptly in a thick rounded end, about an inch below the junction of the left common iliac vein.

CASE III. A pale anæmic girl, æt. 19, was in the hospital on account of excessive debility, and was being dressed by her friends for the purpose of removing her, without regard to the warning which had been given of the danger of such a proceeding, when she fell, fainting, and quickly died. She had been observed, during her stay in the hospital, to lie with the right arm hanging out of bed, and with her head inclined towards the right shoulder; not because she was in pain, but she preferred that position, and could not tell why. In the last few days the arm had swollen. We found the internal organs bloodless, but healthy, with the exception of slight emphysema of the lung. The right innominate, subclavian, and internal jugular veins, were obstructed and distended by a large clot, which, in the innominate vein, was of light or buff colour, scarcely tinged with red, and firm. It was adherent to the coats of the vessel, though easily separated from them; and the internal surface of the vein had lost its polish. In the jugular vein, the interior of the clot was softened to about the consistence of cream, and looked like a mixture of blood and pus. This semifluid portion of the clot was, on all sides, surrounded, and separated from the coats of the vein by a layer of firmer coagulum, which stretched, but was only very loosely adherent to, the vein. The coats of the several veins were natural; but the tissue on their exterior was indurated and infiltrated by serum and lymph.

Case IV. In a man, æt. 45, who died of phthisis, the right upper extremity having, for some days, been œdematous, and the superficial veins of the arm and shoulder distended, we found the subclavian vein, near its junction with the internal jugular, blocked up by a tough brown clot, which was adherent to the interior of the vein. The latter presented no unnatural appearance, except a loss of polish. There was some induration of the tissues on the exterior of the vein. The rest of the subclavian vein, the axillary and the internal jugular, were distended with dark clots; but were in other respects natural. The external jugular was free. There were large, dark, soft clots in the heart; also evidences of recent pleurisy on the right side; and numerous tubercles, and recently formed cavities, in the lungs.

I have met with many similar cases; but it is needless to detail them, because they presented no great differences from those just given, and from others which are to be found in various writings since the time of Morgagni. In some, the deep veins of the calf only were implicated; their condition being evidenced by swelling of the limb, with uneasiness and tenderness in the course of the posterior tibial vessels, and an enlarged, firm, and tender state of the saphena minor. This has occurred lately in two cases, in which I had laid open the tunica vaginalis testis, for the purpose of inducing suppurative inflammation in that membrane. Both the patients were young subjects; one of them was in a debilitated state. In both of them the affection was on the side opposite to that on which the operation had been performed, and subsided spontaneously.

In all the cases that I have seen, with the exception of one of the two just mentioned, the patients have been in a feeble state, most of them having been previously reduced by some other disease. The most frequent causes of the accompanying debility were: some chronic disease, such as phthisis, or a discharging abscess; old age; low fever; or an acute inflammatory affection, more particularly of the serous membranes or of the lungs. In no instance has the condition of the veins appeared to be the cause of death, either directly or indirectly; though in many cases the patients died of the diseases which preceded that condition, and the state of the blood which was induced appeared in some to accelerate the fatal result. It is, moreover, a very important fact, that in no case, which has occurred within my observation or reading, has this affection been productive of any of those alarming and much to be dreaded symptoms, which attend occasionally upon traumatic inflammation of the veins, and occur under other circumstances, and which are supposed to depend upon the admixture of purulent, or other morbid fluids, with the circulating blood. In some instances, as in Case I., the affection is attended with uneasiness, or pain, in the early stages. More commonly, it comes on insidiously and does not attract attention till the swelling of the limb is observed, when some tenderness in the course of the vein may generally be found. Not unfrequently, we are called upon to treat an œdematous state of one of the lower extremities, which commenced during an attack of fever, or some other illness, and which may be traced to an obstruction of the vein that had escaped notice. In several cases the first suspicion of any obstruction to the circulation has been excited by the observation, after death, that one of the limbs was swollen; this has led to an examination of the veins, and to the discovery in them of clots, which must have existed many days.

· The circumstances under which the disease occurs, and the fact that it often affects several parts of the circulatory system at the same time, or consecutively, in the same person, are quite in accordance with the supposition that it depends, primarily, not upon a morbid condition of the vessels, but upon a preternatural tendency to coagulation in the fibrine; and this view derives confirmation from several of the following phenomena, which may be observed in the origin and progress of the malady.

Thus, the obstruction most frequently commences in the parts of the venous system which are most favourable to the coagulation of the blood; viz. in the great veins, particularly those of the lower extremities, where the current is more feeble than in other regions. The points of selection in the lower limbs are: first, at or near the junction of two large veins, as the external and internal iliacs, the superficial and deep femorals, the anterior and posterior tibials; the projecting angles between the confluent trunks, furnishing favourable spots for the settling of the blood: secondly, in the neighbourhood of the valves. These present loose, free edges, to which the fibrine may readily adhere; and each has also the effect of shutting off from the circulating current the small quantity of blood which lies above it, included in the retiring angle, between the upper surface of the valve and the adjacent wall of the vein. The blood so situated must be almost at rest when the circulation is feeble and the limbs are kept quiet, because the valves will be then only partially opened; and, being at rest, it has a favourable opportunity to coagulate and become the nucleus of a larger clot. That this is no imaginary cause is proved by a case in which I found small dry clots lying above—that is, under shelter of—the valves of the femoral vein; the remainder of the vein being free from clots, or nearly so. Moreover, the veins just above the valves often present slight bulgings, or dilatations. Their walls are here a little thicker than at other parts, and they exhibit a faintly reticulated appearance upon the internal surface[1].

It is to be remarked, that the valves are more numerous in the lower limbs than in the upper, and in the deep veins than in the superficial[2]. They are also often placed in the main veins near the points of junction of large branches; so that a number of causes combine to facilitate the coagulation of the blood in these situations.

Thirdly, the formation of the clot often begins in the popliteal vein. This has relation, not merely to the fact that the trunks of the anterior and posterior tibial veins and the saphena minor are here united, but also to the fact that the internal surface of the popliteal vein is often remarkably uneven, presenting quite a reticulated appearance from the

---

[1] In a man, aged 76, who died of senile gangrene, I found a reddish brown clot, which was evidently of many days standing, closely adherent to the valves of the femoral vein, near the junction of the profunda. The rest of the veins, in both lower extremities, were healthy, and contained no peculiar clots.

[2] I have found the distances at which the valves are placed in the *superficial* veins of the lower limbs to be about equal to those at which they are placed in the *deep* veins of the upper limbs.

interlacement of opaque strengthening bands which form projections in the interior.

In the upper part of the body the clots form most frequently
at, or near, the junction of the jugular and subclavian veins,
where there are always large valves, and in the cerebral
sinuses[1]. In the latter, the peculiar construction of their walls
prevents much variation in their calibre, so that there must
be considerable variations in the rate at which the blood
traverses them in different states of the circulation; and they
present, at the points of junction of the branches, many and
marked projecting angles favourable to the settling of the
fibrine.

The clots form not unfrequently in the venous plexuses
around the prostate[2], and in the hæmorrhoidal veins.

It appears that, as a general rule, the formation of the clot
commences on the outside, that is, near to the coats of the
vein, where the current must be somewhat slower than in the
axis of the tube; and the first stage in the process seems to
be the settling of a patch or layer of fibrine upon the inner
surface of the vein. This is probably increased by the addition of successive layers upon the interior, whereby the channel for the blood is diminished. Soon the tube is completely
obstructed; this result being commonly accelerated, more or
less, by the clotting of the blood, in addition to the settling
of the fibrine. The two processes,—fibrinous deposit and
blood-clotting,—which differ, probably, only in the circum-

[1] They were found by Virchow, *Frorieps Notizen*, xxxvii. 30, in the cerebral sinuses, in 6 cases out of 18.

In a remarkable case related by Mr Hulke, *Ophthalmic Reports*, April, 1859,
an obstruction of the left cavernous and adjacent sinuses by coagula was
attended with all the symptoms of aneurism by anastomosis of the orbit, and
the carotid artery was tied by Mr Bowman.

[2] In a man, aged 67, who died with sloughing of the nates, after fracture
of the thigh, I found several short thick firm clots, with stunted branches,
in the veins near the prostate. They were smooth, quite unadherent, and
tumbled out from the divided vessels. A section of each showed a central
cavity containing red fluid, surrounded by a wall composed of tough, laminated, reddish or mottled fibrine. The fluid exhibited red corpuscles and a
great number of pale nucleated cells.

stance that the greater rapidity of the latter causes the entanglement of the red globules with the fibrine, go on somewhat irregularly, whence the mottled appearance of the coagula; but, as a general rule, the clots are firmer and more fibrinous near the exterior, softer and darker in the middle. In a young woman, who died of fever, with peritonitis, excited by approaching perforation of the ilium, we were led to examine the veins by observing some œdema about the left ankle, and found the external and internal iliacs, at and near their junction, on both sides, occupied by coagula, which, on the left side, extended down below the popliteal vein, and, on the right, terminated in an ordinary clot at Poupart's ligament. Sections of these clots showed them to consist of laminated fibrinous tubes, moderately firm, and enclosing central cylinders of dark soft blood. The thickness of the fibrinous tubes varied. In some places, more particularly near the junction of the iliacs, where we judged the affection had commenced, it was so great as to leave little space for the dark central portion of the clot. In other parts, the fibrinous layer was thin; and in one place it was separated from the internal surface of the vein by a layer of soft dark clotted blood, resembling an ordinary recently-formed coagulum in consistence and appearance. This was probably formed from blood, which had insinuated itself between the clot and the vessel, and had coagulated shortly before, or possibly after, death. A transverse section of one of these clots showed very clearly the central dark soft coagulum surrounded by a circle, or tube, of laminated fibrine, which again was enclosed by a more recent dark external layer.

The exterior of the clot is usually smooth; sometimes it has quite a polished appearance, except at the points where it has become adherent to the sides of the vein. These adhesions are not usually very extensive; they are most commonly found where the clot began to form, and vary in their firmness with the period of their duration. The smooth character of the external surface of the clot is important, inasmuch as it rather militates against the view so much advocated by Virchow and some other pathologists, that portions of the clot are very liable to be detached, and to be carried along in the blood-current, till they cause obstruction and give rise to secondary coagula in distant vessels[1].

The extension of the clot in the direction of the heart is usually limited by the junction of some large vein which is sufficient to maintain the current in the main trunk. Often the clot does not reach quite so far as this, but ends on the *peripheral* side of the junction. Thus, when the clot commences at the junction of the iliacs, on one side, it commonly extends about half way up the common iliac; and, in a case of cancer of the uterus, in which the iliacs, on both sides, were obstructed, the clot extended up the vena cava nearly as high as the renal veins. Sometimes the clot reaches further, and terminates in a round or conical end on the *cardiac* side of the point of junction of some large trunk. In the *peripheral* direction it is prolonged to a variable extent into the tributary branches, but does not usually reach the small veins: indeed, the latter are very rarely obstructed, either primarily or secondarily, in this affection.

The clot not only fills and chokes up the vessel, so as to prevent the passage of blood through it, but also distends or stretches it; and this distension, together with a certain amount of irritation resulting from the presence of a solid body in its interior, soon produces an effect upon the walls of the vein, the results of which are exhibited chiefly, or almost exclusively, on the *exterior* of the vessel. Thus we soon find that there is inflammation of the investing cellular tissue, causing an effusion of serum, lymph, or pus; whereas, in the *interior*, there is commonly little change beyond a removal of the epithelium from the lining membrane, and more or less intimate adhesion of the clot to it. There may be also an

[1] Mr Hewitt, *Medico-Chirurgical Transactions*, xxviii. 74, found the clot in one case "enveloped in a perfectly distinct, transparent, smooth, polished membrane, presenting the appearances of serous tissue, with arborescent vessels in its structure."

increase of redness at some parts, which is evidently due to staining by the contiguous blood, inasmuch as it is commonly proportionate to the colour of the contained clot, being deepest where the clot is darkest, and less marked, or quite absent where the clot is composed chiefly of fibrine. I have never seen lymph or pus, or any inflammatory product, formed from the interior of the vein. This proves that the inner coats of veins are by no means easily excited to inflammation, and is quite in accordance with the results of experiments made upon the veins of animals by Lee[1], Mackenzie[1], and Virchow[2]. It accords also with the general results of my experience, which by no means indicate a liability to inflammation in the inner coats of veins. I have, in many instances, applied a ligature to the chief vein of a limb after amputation, without any ill result in a single case; and I have never seen any mischief caused by the ligature of a varicose vein or a hæmorrhoidal tumour, though I have employed that method of treatment very often. It is not improbable that where unfavourable symptoms have ensued in cases of this kind, they have been caused, not so much by inflammation of the vein itself, as by suppuration in the surrounding cellular tissue.

When examining a vein which is plugged by a tough and adhering coagulum, one can scarcely be persuaded that the circulation could ever have been re-established through it, if the patient had survived; yet there can be no doubt that this does take place, and that a vessel may, in process of time, resume its functions, and be restored nearly, if not entirely, to its natural condition, after its channel has been completely, or

---

[1] *Medico-Chirurgical Transactions*, xxxv. and xxxvi. Dr Mackenzie infers, from the results of numerous experiments on the venous system, that the origin of *obstructive* phlebitis is to be sought for in a vitiated state of the blood, that this causes an irritation of the lining membrane of the veins at various points, which, in turn, leads to coagulation of the blood. I do not, however, discover sufficient evidence of this irritation of the lining membrane of the veins, and think there are many reasons against admitting that it is a necessary, or even the ordinary, intermediate link between the vitiated and the coagulated condition of the blood.

[2] *Handbuch der Specielle Pathologie und Therapie*, i. 161.

to a considerable extent, blocked up by a clot. The perfect restoration of the limbs in Case I., and in several other instances, assured me of this; and it is in accordance with the great difficulty which I have experienced in effecting the permanent obliteration of varicose veins by temporary ligatures, or by other means which had for their object the formation of coagula in the vessels. It appears that the blood is almost sure to revert to its natural channel, in process of time, unless the vein be completely destroyed[1]. The dissection in the following case illustrated the condition to which the clots become reduced. A man, aged 63, died, of erysipelas and pleuropneumonia, ten days after resection of one ramus of the lower jaw, performed on account of extensive necrosis and suppuration, which had continued for several months, and had reduced him to a very low state. His health had long been bad; but he did not mention that he had suffered any particular affection of the lower limbs. I was led to examine the veins in consequence of the condition of the pulmonary arteries, presently to be described. In dissecting out the femoral and popliteal vein of the left side, I remarked that the investing layer of cellular tissue, usually so delicate, was more coarse, tough, and closely adherent, than natural. With this exception, there was nothing to attract attention on the exterior of the vessels, or in the structure of their walls. In the interior (see Plate, figs. 1 and 2) were numerous delicate, but tough, white bands or strings, extending across or along the vessels; some were adherent in their whole length, and others only at their ends; also small firm lumps of pale yellow, or gravel, or golden colour, smooth on the surface, and more or less adherent to the inside of the vein. In some places there were merely yellowish stains in the lining membrane of the vein. The nature of these stains would have been scarcely recognisable,

---

[1] Hence in the treatment of varix, where it seems desirable to resort to operative procedure, my practice is to pass a needle or silver wire beneath the vein, and to allow the metal to find its way out by ulceration through the vessel and the superjacent skin.

had they not been in most instances continuous with the threads or some other evident remains of the clots. These veins contained also coagula, which appeared to have been formed recently, probably after death. The popliteal and lower part of the femoral vein, on the right side, presented appearances similar to those on the left. The upper part of the femoral vein was occupied by a firm, dry, mottled clot; and the profunda was tightly plugged by a continuation of the same, of white colour. Above the junction of the profunda, the vein was distended by a clot of comparatively recent formation, which, in the centre, was semifluid and of dirty cream colour. This soft part contained red corpuscles, and larger pale cells having indistinct nuclei.

It is no uncommon thing for the middle part of the clot to be, as in this instance, softened and converted into a dirty pultaceous or creamy substance, in which corpuscles are found, varying in size and shape, less regularly formed than pus-cells, and having less distinct nuclei. These are intermixed with oil-globules and red corpuscles; the latter may be natural in appearance, or more or less misshapen and granulated, and in various stages of dissolution. The changes which the blood thus undergoes are, as it would appear from the experiments of Mr Gulliver[1], similar to those which take place when it is subjected to concoction after its removal from the body. They seem most frequently to occur when the clot has been quickly formed.

In all the cases that I have seen, except one, the soft central part of the clot was walled in by the firmer exterior portion, so that there was no opportunity for any of the *débris* to enter the circulating current.

The exceptional instance was that of a sickly lad who died in a state of extreme emaciation, with bed-sores, &c. after amputation of the right knee. The left femoral vein was blocked up and distended by a clot which was slightly

---

[1] *Medico-Chirurgical Transactions*, xxii. 138.

adherent to the interior of the vessel and presented the appearances usual in such cases. It extended into the external iliac
and terminated, near the upper end of that vessel, in a soft
semifluid dirty substance, which had been free, so far as we
could discover, to mix with the fluid blood in the common
iliac and vena cava. If any barrier had existed it was broken
down, before, or after, death, and had disappeared. The lad
had suffered under inflammation and swelling of several joints,
attended with perspirations and rigors, subsequent to the amputation; and a small abscess had formed near the left ankle.
These, however, had all subsided before the commencement
of that swelling in the leg, which indicated an obstruction in
the vein; and there were no symptoms in the latter part of his
illness, and no appearances after death, to justify the supposition that the blood had suffered from the admixture of
morbid matter.

The right femoral vein in this same patient was contracted
and converted into a firm white cord. Its canal was impervious to fluid; but I succeeded in pushing a probe along it,
and, on cutting it open, found it occupied by a tenacious
yellowish white substance not unlike putty. This, which
I judged to be altered fibrine or blood, was seen under the
microscope to be composed of granules of various sizes. The
external and common iliac veins were also impervious. The
outline of the former was not very distinct, its track being
occupied by a quantity of yellowish white substance similar
to that in the femoral vein; and some of this substance was in
contact with the fibres of the psoas muscle, the coats of the
vessel having disappeared. Doubtless these veins had, at a
former period, been in a condition more or less similar to those
on the left side; and they offered an example of the changes
which may take place after the clot has been so softened and
connected with the walls of the vein as to cause the obliteration of the vessel [1].

---

[1] There was a similar condition of the veins in a case described by Dr R.
Lee, *Med.-Ch. Trans.* xv. 137. Specimen 1733 in the Museum of the College

It seems probable that the softening of these clots may sometimes give rise to the formation of abscesses. But I have never been able to prove that it does so. We not unfrequently meet with abscesses containing pus and blood in the course of the superficial veins of the lower extremities in persons who are in a low or disordered state of health; and such abscesses are supposed to originate in the vessels, and to be due to the softening of coagula found in them. In one

of Surgeons offers an example of a further result of the same process. It is thus described in the Catalogue: "The right iliac veins with the surrounding parts. Parts of them appear to have been completely obstructed by clots in which bone-like matter has been formed." "The whole length of the left external iliac vein is obliterated and contracted, and its coats are slightly distended, thickened and indurated. In its interior there is an appearance of the coagulum of blood by which it was probably at first obstructed, and which has now lost its colour and become firm and completely adherent to the inner surface of the vein." They were taken from the Earl of Liverpool, who had a swelling of the left leg and thigh, and a varicose state of the veins from the ankle to the groin, for several years before death.

Cases of obliteration of the veins, some of which were probably from similar causes, are given and referred to in Hodgson's *Treatise on the Arteries and Veins*, p. 525.

The appearances in the following case are interesting; though it may not be clear how far they are to be connected with one another. A young woman died of phthisis. There was nothing to create suspicion of any disease in the veins. On the inner surface of the lower part of the vena cava was an opake-white slightly raised patch, tolerably well defined, of the size of a fourpenny-piece. The surrounding interior of the vein presented radiating lines indicative of some contraction having taken place. The patch was quite smooth, of tough structure, and consisted of fibres, some of which resembled those of elastic tissue, others were straight and parallel, and others, rather thicker and less clearly defined, were nucleated. At the junction of the iliacs, on the left side, the lining membrane was rather thickened, of opake-white or yellowish colour, and slightly reticulated, forming a patch resembling that in the vena cava, but larger and less well-defined. There was also a similar appearance of radiation, in the interior of the vessel, around it. Though the blood was fluid in most other parts there was a large dark clot in this situation, having the appearance of a clot formed after death. In the right femoral vein, lying under the shelter of one of the valves, between it and the side of the vessel, was a small, dry, firm, mottled clot just fitted to the niche which it occupied. It had evidently been formed some time before death, and it was slightly adherent to the side of the vein. While the vessels were being removed a firm cylindrical clot fell out from the profunda vein. It was about two inches long, conical at the ends, dry, with a smooth surface, and was composed of dark and white portions alternating irregularly.

B

case, however, of the kind the patient died; and I dissected carefully without being able to discover any communication, or connection, between the several abscesses and sinuses and the trunk or branches of the saphena vein over or near which they were situated; neither was there any evidence of clots having formed in these vessels.

We come next to inquire what are the conditions of the blood which predispose it thus to coagulate in the veins during life. It has been already remarked, that the clots are most liable to form in persons who are in an enfeebled and cachectic state. Now, in this state, it is well known that the fibrine of the blood exceeds its normal proportions; and it appears that its tendency to coagulation is increased by there being also in the blood an excess of water, which dilutes the saline or ammoniacal elements, and thereby renders them less able to hold the fibrine in solution. Nevertheless, persons often remain in cachectic and anæmic states for a great length of time; and they may, in addition, suffer several and prolonged attacks of syncope, without any coagulation of the blood taking place. Indeed, the cases in which the latter occurs are quite the exception; and we therefore search for some other cause to explain the phenomenon in these exceptional instances. It is most frequent when the cachexia has been induced by some inflammatory affection; and we know that the effect of inflammation, more particularly when it attacks the serous membranes, is to increase the amount and the coagulability of the fibrine. The parturient state, which, especially in the early period of lactation, is productive of a similar effect upon the blood, is also marked by a great tendency to clotting of the blood in the venous system. The researches of Dr Richardson[1], continued with great assiduity and care through a long period, give strong reason for his view that the fibrine is held in solution by the presence of ammonia, and that its tendency to coagulate in the body is increased, and its coagulation out of the body is accelerated, by a diminution of the volatile alkali of the blood;

[1] *The Cause of the Coagulation of the Blood*, 1858.

and it is quite probable that, in the cases which we are dis-
cussing, an insufficient quantity of this solvent medium is one
of the proximate causes leading to the clotting of the blood
in the vessels[1]. There may be, in addition, some alteration
in those relations of the corpuscles to one another and to the
walls of the vessels, which, though not well understood, have
an important influence in facilitating the circulation of the
blood[2]. Certainly there seems no good reason to attribute
the affection to the introduction of pus or other morbid fluid
into the circulating current.

The diagnosis of the disease is easy. Œdema of the limb
is often the first symptom. This may be attended with, or
preceded by, uneasiness in the course of the affected vessels;
and there is enlargement of the superficial veins, with, perhaps, induration of some of them. When the femoral vein is
affected, the inner side of the thigh is sometimes swollen in a
marked manner. The integuments usually remain white;
occasionally they are inflamed in patches, or in a more diffused
manner; and occasionally they are mottled by purplish spots,
like petechial spots, or like those resulting from ecchymosis.
Mortification rarely or never results from this cause alone[3].

I have already said that the affection is rarely attended

---

[1] The researches of Scherer and Lehmann (*Physiological Chemistry*, i. 97)
show that the blood sometimes exhibits an acid reaction in the puerperal state ;
the acid present is supposed to be the lactic. This may be associated with the
fact that the skin may be often observed to be remarkably dry in cases in which
the blood coagulates in the vessels during life. An incipient decomposition of
the blood is regarded by Zimmermann to be one of the chief causes of its
coagulation.

[2] The commencement of the clots must be attributed to influences affecting
the fibrine, rather than the corpuscles, because at the parts where they are first
formed they are usually composed almost entirely of fibrine. Nevertheless, it
is most probable that changes in one of the constituents of the blood are
attended with corresponding alterations in the others ; and the analogy that
may be drawn from what is observed in inflammation and in pregnancy, sug-
gests that an increase in the coagulating tendency of the fibrine is accompanied
by an increase in the adhesive qualities of the corpuscles, which would mate-
rially contribute to the formation of clots, and which may, indeed, sometimes
be the immediately originating cause of them.

[3] Virchow, *Handbuch der Speciellen Pathologie und Therapie*, i. 171.

with any serious consequences. It does not commonly seem much to aggravate the patient's condition, or to diminish his chance of recovery: indeed, I have sometimes observed an amelioration in the general condition of the patient to be coincident with the swelling of a limb which indicated an obstruction in the great vein; as though the general mass of the blood had become thereby relieved of a certain quantity of its redundant fibrine, and was consequently better fitted to minister to the healthy nutrition of the body. If the obstruction of a vein occur during the course of an inflammatory disease, it generally takes place when the disease is subsiding: it may, therefore, be regarded as an attendant on recovery, though it is an evidence of a low or cachectic state of system. I may again remark, that it seems to have no relation to the malady called " pyæmia;" and though necropsies prove that it is sometimes associated with the formation of clots in the pulmonary arteries, I have not in any case had clinical evidence of its being followed by that formidable affection.

Nevertheless, it is a dispiriting, tedious malady; it retards the restoration of the patient, keeps him confined to his bed, and causes much annoyance and apprehension. The liability to its occurrence is to be borne in mind as a reason against having recourse to depletion or purgation, or other measures which may exhaust the patient, or draw away the saline and watery ingredients of the blood, in the latter stages of an inflammatory or febrile affection. I have given ammonia in some cases in which I thought there might be a predisposition to the formation of clots; and, where the general condition of the patient is likely to be benefited by the use of such a medicine, we should not ignore the evidences which have been afforded of its influence in retarding coagulation of the fibrine. If given in a pure form, it is probable that some of it will enter the blood; and that it will operate in the living vessels, more or less, in the same manner as it is found to do when mixed with blood which has been removed from the body. When the blood has begun to clot in the veins of a limb

I do not think that much good results from any particular local treatment. The affection runs a certain course, and, if the disease upon which it is an attendant do not prove fatal, will gradually subside spontaneously; and the veins usually become clear again. Considering the nature and cause of the malady, we should be unwilling to resort to the use of leeches. Nevertheless, I have known decided relief follow their application when the pain and inflammation around the vein was considerable. Fomentations are sometimes attended with comfort.

Of the instances which I have seen, the greater number have been in males[1]. Nevertheless, it appears to be the same condition of the veins which in women, after delivery, usually constitutes the disease known by the name of "phlegmasia dolens." The cause of the disease, and the results disclosed by dissection, appear to correspond very closely, whether it be developed after parturition, or in the course of an illness; and the name "phlegmasia dolens in the male" has, accordingly, been applied to it by Sir H. Halford[2] and others. Phlegmasia dolens most frequently occurs *after* parturition, at that time when the fibrine of the blood is found to be most abundant; viz. during the early period of lactation; and it is most common in women who are weak at the time of delivery, or whose strength has been reduced by flooding, and especially in those in whom there has been, in addition, peritonitis or some inflammatory affection of the chest. Moreover, when a fatal result has followed, it has commonly resulted, not from the condition of the veins, but from some other cause[3]. It must, however, be observed that, in phleg-

[1] Of forty non-puerperal cases tabulated by Dr Mackenzie (*Medico-Chirurgical Transactions*, xxxvi. 235), about two-thirds were females, and one-third males.

[2] *Medical Gazette*, x. 172.

[3] See paper by Dr Davis, who first pointed out the true nature of this disease, *Medico-Chirurgical Transactions*, vol. xii.; also papers by other writers in the same *Transactions*, and in various medical journals. Dr Simpson, in his lectures recently published in the *Medical Times and Gazette*, calls attention to the fact that in some well-marked cases of phlegmasia dolens the veins have been found quite healthy.

masia dolens, the pain is usually more severe, and the disease, on the whole, is of a more acute nature than in the ordinary obstruction of the veins: it seems sometimes to originate in a morbid condition of the uterine veins, and is sometimes attended with, or productive of, those inflammatory and suppurative affections in distant parts which are attributed to a morbid condition of the blood.

Indeed, phlegmasia dolens would seem to occupy an intermediate position between the simple and comparatively innocent obstruction of the veins, which we have been considering, and the more severe and dangerous affection of the veins, which has been described by Arnott[1], and others, as an occasional attendant upon wounds and injuries. The changes which occur in the veins, and in the blood contained in them, seem to be much the same in the three classes of cases, except that in the traumatic variety the inflammatory symptoms are commonly more severe. And there is the further important difference, that in it we are liable to encounter that alarming, and commonly fatal, train of symptoms which is supposed to depend upon a purulent infection of the blood; whereas, in the ordinary obstruction of the veins, as I have already said, such concomitants are little to be apprehended.

The purport of the foregoing remarks may be condensed into the following summary :

1. The great veins are very liable to become obstructed by clots forming in them when the patient is greatly debilitated, and when the circulation is enfeebled—by inflammatory affections, by discharging abscesses, difficult labours, and other causes.

---

[1] *Medico-Chirurgical Transactions*, xv. 46. Mr Arnott remarks, and I think he was the first to call attention to the fact, that the inflammatory changes "are usually limited by the passage of a current of blood ; where a trunk is concerned, the boundary line being the entrance of a branch, and where a branch is concerned, the boundary being the junction of this with the trunk."

2. The clots result from an altered state of the blood, disposing the fibrine to solidify; and are found in those parts of the veins which offer the greatest facilities for its so doing.

3. The inflammation of the veins is a consequence of the presence of the clot, and is chiefly confined to their outer coats, and to the surrounding cellular tissue.

4. The clots may soften and become intimately connected with the walls of the vessels, and may lead to the complete and permanent obliteration of their canals: more commonly, however, they are removed, or shrink into delicate bands or fibres, which offer little or no obstruction to the circulation.

5. The affection rarely leads to any serious result. It may be associated with so-called pyæmia; but has no necessary or frequent connection with it.

II.—Clots in the Pulmonary Artery.

The following examples of this affection have come under my notice.

Case I. A thin, delicate lady, aged about 35, was confined with her third child, and had so quick and easy a time that the medical attendant, who lived close by, was not summoned. No unfavourable symptoms followed till the fourteenth day, when, having been nursing her infant, she went into an adjoining room, and whilst in the act of standing up to pour out tea, she suddenly fell back upon the sofa, as if faint, and died. The pulmonary arteries, on both sides, where they enter the lungs, were plugged with dark clots of moderately firm consistence. These were not of uniform colour, some parts being darker than others; and they did not appear to have formed long before death. They extended into the second divisions of the arteries, and were only slightly adherent to the walls of the vessels. The latter were quite healthy. The lungs, heart, and other great organs, and the blood in them and in other parts of the body, presented nothing remarkable.

CASE II. An exceedingly fat woman, aged 54, had been confined to her room three weeks by a sore leg, and in the last few days had suffered three attacks of dyspnœa and faintness, for which ammonia had been given by her medical attendant. One of these occurred on the 21st of the month, and she felt very ill all that day. On the 22nd she was better. On the 23rd, being in a neighbouring house, I was summoned to her in consequence of a sudden seizure, and was in time only to see her die. There were a few inspirations, but I could not feel the pulse. When first attacked, a few minutes before her death, she was quite sensible, and said, " It's of no use; I'm dying." The main branches of the pulmonary artery, on both sides, were distended with firm, dark, mottled clots, which extended into the second and third divisions of the artery. The interior of the vessel was discoloured, but for the most part it preserved its polish. In a few places, where the clots were slightly adherent, it had lost somewhat of its natural smoothness. In other respects it was quite healthy. The substance of the lungs was natural. The walls of the heart were flabby and thin; but the muscular structure and the valves were healthy. The right auricle and ventricle were distended with clots which were large, firm, and fibrinous in their upper parts.

CASE III. A girl, aged about 18, had been in service in the town, in a hard place, under a hard mistress, had been ailing for several days, had one or two fainting fits, and in the last few days, had suffered from shortness of breath, and other symptoms which excited suspicion of inflammation of the lungs. When she was admitted into the hospital she had an anæmic appearance, her breathing was quick and hurried, and her manner was suggestive of hysteria, rather than real disease, to the gentleman who then saw her. Next day a faint abnormal sound was thought to be audible about the base of the heart; ten minims of tincture of digitalis were prescribed. At six o'clock that day, just after the bowels had been relieved in bed, the bed-pan being used, she fainted, and died before the house-surgeon could reach the ward. The left pulmonary artery contained a tough clot, tightly impacted in the main trunk, with prolongations extending into the third and fourth branches. It was party-coloured, with alternating black and white portions, quite free and smooth in the smaller branches of the vessel; but in the first and second divisions it adhered at some points to the lining membrane so as to require slight pressure with the handle of the scalpel to detach it. The vessel appeared to have lost its epithelium at these points, and presented some patches of red. The right pulmonary artery was still more tightly plugged with a tough, dry, party-coloured clot, which was adherent to about the first and second divisions of the vessel, and was at this part softened in its middle to a considerable extent. The heart and the large vessels of the trunk and extremities were healthy. The clots in the venous system were rather larger and firmer than usual, but appeared to have been all formed after death. The contiguous parts of the upper and lower lobes of the right lung were consolidated by pneumonia, and covered with lymph.

CASE IV. An emaciated young man had for several weeks suffered under symptoms of abdominal and pulmonary phthisis, with feverishness and diarrhœa. He was reduced to a very low state, and was slowly dying for some days. There were tubercles in the peritoneum, and in both lungs. In the pulmonary artery of one lung was a large, firm, fibrinous clot, nearly filling the vessel, with prolongations extending into its third and fourth divisions. It was slightly adherent about the point where the artery first divides; and the interior of the vessel, at this part, was rather rough and reddish when the clot had been removed. At the corresponding situation in the other pulmonary artery was a mottled clot of darker colour, and apparently more recent. It was slightly adherent to the vessel, and its prolongations extended into the large branches. The left lower extremity was œdematous, and the femoral and profunda veins and their tributaries were distended with dark, mottled clots, which were slightly adherent about the neighbourhood of the valves. Neither the coats of the vessels, nor the investing tissue, had undergone any change. In the profunda, two valves were adherent together; and a narrow, tough bridle, of yellowish colour, passed from them to the adjacent side of the vein. It looked as if it were the remnant of a clot which had formed at some previous period.

CASE V. A lad, aged 12, died, much emaciated, with disease of the hip and discharging abscesses. The left pulmonary artery was extensively occupied by clots. These, in the larger branches, were light coloured and soft; in the smaller branches they were darker, more mottled, tougher and drier; in neither were they adherent to the lining membrane, except in one situation where a vessel looked as if converted into a long narrow abscess. There was no other disease in the lungs. Well formed coagula, of the usual character, and some fluid blood, were found in the cavities of the heart. The lower part of one external iliac vein, with the femoral and profunda veins, were blocked up by coagula, which were closely adherent in the vicinity of the valves.

CASE VI. An old man died exhausted, after suffering retention of urine for some time, which required the frequent use of the catheter. The left lower extremity was swollen; and the great veins were distended with clots from the junction with the right iliac, where the clot terminated abruptly, to low down in the leg. They appeared to have commenced where the profunda joins the femoral. In the left pulmonary artery, where it divides into its primary branches, was a small, toughish, slightly mottled clot, adhering to the lining membrane, which was very slightly altered.

CASE VII. In the patient who died after removal of a portion of the lower jaw, followed by erysipelas and pneumonia, whose case has been before referred to (page 14), the trunk and primary branches of the right pulmonary artery (fig. 3) were nearly filled up by a firm, yellowish white, fibrinous clot, which was for the most part loosely adherent to the vessels, but in some places was so firmly attached that the lining membrane was torn up in the attempts to detach it. In the smaller branches of the artery the clot was mottled with red and white portions, was less adherent, but was firm and dry, and filled up the canal. Its ramifications extended as far as I could follow them. The lower lobe of the lung was hepatised; and there was sero-purulent fluid in the pleural cavity. The trunk and primary branches of the left pulmonary artery (fig. 4) were occupied by a still firmer and older clot, which was white, quite closely adherent to one side of the vessel, so as to form a part of its wall; and the smooth surface of the clot was continuous with that of the artery. Though the new structure stood out in strong relief, and occupied a considerable space of the canal, there was still room enough for a large column of blood. The ramification of this clot in the secondary and tertiary branches of the artery were closely adherent to the sides of the vessel, so as to form mere ridge-like projections, which would not have much interfered with the current of blood. They were marked with dark lines and spots, as if from deposit of pigment in them. In some of the branches of the artery the only remaining trace of the clot was a staining of the lining membrane with delicate dark lines. These stains were continuous with the clots which occupied the larger branches. There was no apparent disease of the vessel itself. The lower lobe of this lung was in a pneumonic state.

There can, I think, be little doubt that the formation of the clots in the pulmonary arteries, in these, and other like cases[1],

[1] Baron, *Archives Générales de Médecine*, ii. p. 1, appears first to have directed attention to the subject. Paget, *Medico-Chirurgical Transactions*,

is due to the same causes as the formation of the clots in the great veins; that is to say, it is due, primarily, to an increase in the coagulative tendency of the fibrine of the blood, and, secondarily, to some facilities which the vessel offers for that coagulation to take place. With regard to the primary cause: the pulmonary clots have been found chiefly, if not exclusively, in cases where the vital powers have been lowered by some other disease; in short, in cachectic states, especially where an inflammatory affection was superadded; and after confinements; that is, in precisely the same conditions as the venous clots. Moreover, the clots are often found in both situations in the same patient, as in Cases IV. V. VI. and VII.[1]

With regard to the secondary, or immediately inducing cause: it has not been satisfactorily shown in any one instance that the clot was preceded by, or attributable to, disease in the coats of the vessel. The discoloration and roughening, where they were present, was evidently due, as in the case of the veins, to the presence of the clot, and were not the cause of it[2].

It appears, from the above related cases, and others which have been recorded, that the clots begin to form, in some instances, in the smaller branches of the vessels; and that in these instances there is often some obstruction to the circulation in the artery, caused by inflammation, pulmonary apoplexy, or other cause, which must tend to promote the settling of the fibrine. In other cases the affection commences in the

---

ix. and x. Ormerod, *Medical Gazette.* Virchow, *Archiv,* x. 225. (In the case related here, the blood in the heart was fluid), and *Handbuch der Speciellen Pathologie,* Bd. i.

[1] Virchow, *Frorieps Notizen,* xxxviii. 35, remarks that in only one case out of eleven, in which clots were found in the pulmonary arteries, did he fail to discover them in some other part of the venous system.

[2] Kidd, *Dublin Journal of Medical Science,* xxii. 376, attributes the affection to inflammation of the pulmonary artery. Baron alludes to the absence of an inflammatory condition of the vessel in the case described by him. Nevertheless, in some other cases, to which he refers, he conceives that inflammation of the wall of the vessel led to the formation of the clots.

larger branches, or in the main trunk; and in these the spot at which the first deposit takes place is usually at or near the root of the lung. In this situation the pulmonary artery breaks up at once into a number of branches, which radiate from it, at different angles, to the several parts of the lung. Consequently, a large extent of surface is presented to the blood, and there are numerous angular projections into the current; both which conditions are calculated to induce the coagulation of the fibrine. It must also be remembered that the rate at which the blood travels through the pulmonary arteries is subject to considerable variations, depending, partly upon the alternating contraction and repose, and the varying force of the contraction, of the right ventricle, and partly upon the vicissitudes of respiration; and both these sources of disturbance become more marked in those enfeebled states, with tendency to fainting, in which we have found that the fibrine has a peculiar disposition to settle. In such states the circulation in the vessel must always be feeble; and, probably, the current is sometimes absolutely suspended in certain portions of the artery, or in the main trunk, for short periods. Moreover, the venous blood seems to exhibit an increasing disposition to coagulate in the body as it approaches the lungs, and therefore may be presumed to acquire the property in the greatest degree in the pulmonary arteries.

At any rate, the clots which we find in ordinary *post-mortem* examinations are more common and larger in these vessels, and in the right cavities of the heart, than in any other parts of the body. Frequently they are of firm consistence, while the blood in the other veins, and in the left side of the heart, is quite fluid.

Virchow attributes the formation of these plugs in the pulmonary arteries to the lodgment there of small clots, or fragments of clots ("emboli") which have been formed in the veins, and have been wafted, with the blood, through the right cavities of the heart, towards the lungs. These fragments, he thinks, become detached from the ends of the clots which project into the great venous trunks; thus, in any case, where the end of a clot, formed in one iliac vein, projected into the vena cava, a portion may be washed off by the blood flowing against it from the other iliac vein, and, being carried into the pulmonary artery, may lodge upon one of the projecting angles of the vessel, and constitute a nucleus for the formation of a plug. It is not improbable that this may sometimes occur. It must, however, be remembered that the surface of the venous clots is usually quite smooth, and therefore not very likely to be disintegrated by the slowly flowing current of blood; secondly, that in many cases, as in No. I. II. III. there was no reason to suppose that the pulmonary clots were preceded by clots in the veins; and thirdly, that the effects of a preternatural tendency of the venous blood to coagulate are, for the reasons just given, likely to be exhibited in the pulmonary arteries as well as in other parts of the system.

The pulmonary clots undergo the same changes as those in the veins, provided the patient survives. They may soften (Cases III. and V.)[1] or become firmly adherent to the vessel and disappear, leaving scarcely a trace behind (as in Case VII.); or be converted into threads or bands, stretching from one part of the tube to another. I do not know an instance in which they have caused obliteration of any of the pulmonary vessels; though it is probable that this may take place occasionally in the smaller branches.

The plugging with coagula does not appear to induce inflammation on the exterior of the pulmonary arteries so easily as it does in the case of the veins of the limbs. It is not usually attended with pain or uneasiness, or any symptoms which lead, with certainty, to a diagnosis. Hurried, oppressed breathing, with faintness, occurring without any other obvious cause, would make us suspicious of this affection, and should induce us to auscultate in the situations in which a bruit,

---

[1] In the case related by Dr Kidd, *loc. cit.*, one of the clots was softened in the middle, and the tissues around the artery, on one side, were condensed and indurated.

originating in the pulmonary arteries, would be most likely to be distinguished. I am not aware that a bruit, produced in this manner, has yet been recognised, though it probably would have been discovered had attention been directed to the point during the life of any of the patients.

It is, indeed, a remarkable feature in the affection that the pulmonary arteries, one or both, in the main trunks, or in the larger branches, may be blocked up to a considerable extent without causing any sign of obstruction to the circulation, or of affection of the lungs, or, indeed, without producing any symptom whatever. In Case VII. it was clear, from the size of its remains, that a clot must at some time have occupied nearly the entire calibre of the main trunk of each of the pulmonary arteries; yet there had been no symptom of such condition observed during the life of the patient. In Case I. the patient appeared to be in her usual health till the moment of the fatal seizure. In this, and other parallel cases that have been recorded, there can be no doubt that the clots were forming for some time before death, and that sufficient blood found its way by the side of them into the lungs to maintain the circulation and supply the wants of the system.

The sudden death is probably caused by a slight exertion following a period of repose. During the repose we may judge that the clots are increasing; and the ensuing exertion, by causing a greater demand for oxygenated blood than can be supplied through the impeded pulmonary vessels, induces fainting, which is fatal. The extreme suddenness of the fatal seizure in these cases has suggested the idea that it may have been caused by some displacement of the clots, producing more complete occlusion of the vessels; but this is opposed by the fact that the clots are usually more or less adherent to the walls of the vessels, and show no sign of such displacement having taken place.

III.—CLOTS IN THE CEREBRAL SINUSES.

A girl, æt. 15, in whom the catamenia had never appeared, suffered headache for several days, and had been attended by a medical man, who thought the affection to be of hysterical nature. I saw her on March 7th. She had a dull heavy expression and an obstinate manner. The mouth was firmly closed; and she could not, or would not, put out her tongue or answer questions; yet she was evidently conscious of what passed and showed a certain amount of cunning. She did not appear to be able to use the left arm or leg, and when out of bed did not put the left leg to the ground; but when the soles were tickled she drew up both legs alike. The breathing was noisy. Head to be shaved; Aperient given and Hydr. Chlor. gr. ij every four hours. On the 8th the countenance was more dull and heavy, the eyes vacantly staring; when left alone she fell into a heavy sleep. Urine passed into the bed. P. 110 rather sharp.—Acetum Canth: and Empl: Canth: capiti. On the 9th she was rather less drowsy and took some notice, still did not move left arm or leg. After this the drowsiness increased to stupor; the pupils became rather dilated, and the optic axes ceased to converge; a slight tremor occasionally pervaded the frame; she became weaker, and the pulse became quicker. She died on the 11th.

Examination next day. Dura mater and arachnoid natural. Pacchionian glands larger and more grey than usual. On the right side of brain the convolutions were rather compressed and dry: on the left there was more than the usual amount of fluid in the pia mater. The ventricles contained a considerable quantity of fluid, which had evidently been recently effused, for the septum lucidum was torn through, and the lining of the cavities was in other places ragged. The interior of both ventricles was, moreover, studded with numerous red spots, averaging about the size of a pin's head. These were most abundant in the right ventricle, and especially on the surface of the optic thalamus. An incision into that body disclosed a red patch in its middle, of about the size of a nutmeg, composed of a vast number of minute points of congestion or extravasation, so closely set, especially near the centre, as to give it almost the look of an apoplectic clot. We could not tell whether the appearance was entirely due to distension of the vessels, or whether there was extravasation in addition. Towards the circumference the red points were more separate. In the corresponding part of the left optic thalamus was a similar, but smaller and less deeply coloured, patch. A more or less ecchymosed appearance pervaded the remainder of the optic thalami, the corpora striata, and the adjacent substance of the brain. It was also present to some extent all over the grey matter of the right side of the cerebrum and the cerebellum, and in some parts of the left side; and there were spots of the same in various parts of the white substance of both hemispheres. We were struck by the appearance of the venæ Galeni, which were greatly distended with firm, mottled, slightly adhering clots. The same condition existed in the straight sinus and in the right cavernous, petrosal, and lateral sinuses. It was in some places difficult to detach the clots; and the lining membrane of the sinuses had, in these situations, lost its polish and was excoriated. Some of the veins on the surface of the hemisphere were blocked up with mottled coagula. The right jugular vein was healthy. The lateral and other sinuses on the left side and the longitudinal sinus were healthy.

It seems most probable that the blocking up of the sinuses was the earliest of the morbid phenomena, and that the others were dependent upon it; but what should have caused a deposition of fibrine to take place in these vessels is not clear[1].

---

[1] A similar case is related by Dr Bright, *Medical Reports*, ii. 57. Patient was a child, æt. 20 months, who had recently had pneumonia. Also cases by Dr J. W. Ogle, *Transactions of Pathological Society*, vi. 31, and in the last

IV.—ON THE CLOTTING OF THE BLOOD IN THE CAVITIES OF THE HEART.

In the following case the evidences of the formation of clots in the cavities of the heart and in the blood-vessels were unusually clear; and there can be little doubt that death was due to this cause.

A delicate girl, aged 11, was received into the hospital, March 27th, 1859, with a burn upon the outer surface of the right thigh, and on the palmar aspect of the right forearm. The skin was destroyed over a considerable extent; but it was hoped that she would recover, and, for several days, the wounds proceeded favourably, under the application of flour. About April 8th, without any apparent cause, she became rather feverish and refused her food. The slight feverishness subsided, but left her very feeble, with small pulse, dryish tongue, and shrivelled, harsh, scaling skin, the finger-ends feeling as after scarlet fever. Wine and nutritious diet were administered, and some improvement took place. On the morning of the 17th she was very low, but enjoyed her meals more than on previous days; and the nurse thought her better. About four in the afternoon she was somewhat uneasy, and begged the nurse to sit by her; but nothing remarkable was observed till about two hours afterwards, when she asked to be raised up in the bed. As soon as this request had been complied with, it was perceived that she was dying, and in a few minutes she was dead. No marked difficulty of breathing or other especial symptoms were noticed.

Fifteen hours after death we found the right cavities of the heart, the left ventricle, and all the vessels connected with these cavities, filled with fibrinous clots. The left auricle also con-

volume. In one the fibrinous clot in the sinus was attributed to asthenia, and in a second to disease of the internal ear; in a third it was associated with suppurative pneumonia.

tained a clot, but was not filled by it. The central and greater parts of the clots presented the ordinary characters of the fibrinous masses often found in the heart, though they were tougher and firmer than usual. They were not laminated. Under the microscope they exhibited very fine linear fibres, disposed in an irregular network. The exterior of the clots presented, however, in many places, quite a different appearance. It had a more opaque white, or cream colour, something like lymph in the neighbourhood of an abscess, and was composed, apparently throughout, of well formed cells, larger, clearer, and less granulated than pus-cells, with distinct nuclei. This cream-coloured portion of the clot was, in the right auricle, separated by a defined line from the remaining buff-coloured part, and could easily be peeled off from it. It had not quite a smooth external surface, and adhered slightly to the interior of the cavity, particularly in the appendix; nevertheless, it remained with the clot when the latter was turned out of the auricle. In the ventricles it adhered to the lining membrane of the heart more closely than in the auricles, especially about the edges of the valves, and near the apices of the cavities, prolongations of it being intertwined with the carneæ columnæ. Where the clots extended into the pulmonary artery and aorta, they were deeply impressed by the sigmoid valves; but were not adherent to them.

Near the bifurcation of the pulmonary artery the whole thickness of the clot had a dull cream colour, and this was the case in the primary divisions of the vessel. In no place were the clots adherent to the walls of the pulmonary artery. Fibrinous strings, presenting the usual appearance, extended into the smaller branches of the artery.

In the inferior cava and the iliac veins was some fluid blood, which coagulated on exposure to the air. There were mingled with it numerous small clots, coloured in different degrees: some of these were particoloured. They appeared to be free in the fluid blood, or, if adherent to the walls of the vessels, their connexion was very slight. In the great veins which converge to the superior cava, the clots were more numerous, larger, and more fibrinous, but still loose in the tubes, or very slightly connected with their walls. The left jugular and subclavian veins, at and near their junction, were almost filled by yellowish or cream-coloured clots, having a peculiar coiled or wrinkled exterior (fig. 5), which must have been caused by their being subject to some movements during the flow of the blood, or to their having been formed, or increased, by smaller clots carried in the current from other parts, and intercepted there. None of the vessels were distended by the clots.

In all the arteries which I examined, except the aorta and pulmonary arteries, the blood was fluid. The heart itself was quite sound, and there was no disease of the internal organs.

I have seen other cases more or less similar. In none of them, however, did the symptoms and the appearances after death so clearly indicate that death had been caused by the clotting of the blood in the cavities of the heart and in the adjacent great vessels. Such cases form a highly important class, to which the attention of pathologists and practical men is being more and more closely directed, and for the clear appreciation and discrimination of which much information as to the causes influencing and regulating the coagulation of the blood within the body, before and after death, has yet to be sought. At present, I think we are unable to explain many of the appearances we are in the habit of observing, and of deciding with certainty whether they are to be referred to *post-mortem* changes, or whether they commenced during the life of the patients. For instance, we often find the cavities of the heart (the right auricle and ventricle more particularly, the left ventricle not unfrequently, the left auricle more rarely) filled with fibrinous clots, and the prolongations of the clots extending into the adjacent vessels and descending into the most dependent branches of the pulmonary arteries; so that the absence of colour in them does not admit of explanation upon the ordinarily received hypothesis of the subsidence of the red corpuscles during the slow coagulation which goes on in the recently dead body, because the lowermost portions of the clots in the several cavities, and the most dependent portions in the pulmonary arteries, are as devoid of colour as the uppermost parts. Nevertheless, it seems pretty certain that clots of this kind are, for the most part, formed after death. Coincident with these fibrinous clots is sometimes a variable amount of fluid blood, which may be in the same cavities as the clots; commonly there is some fluid blood in the left auricle. Not unfrequently the clots extending from the ventricles into the pulmonary artery and the aorta exhibit well marked impressions of the semilunar valves, showing clearly that they were moulded upon the valves; and this is regarded as evidence of their having been formed before death[1]. Yet these clots are almost invariably found not adherent to the valves, but quite free from them and smooth. Moreover, each one commonly bears the impression of each of the three valves in an equal degree; and this often happens on both sides of the heart in the same body. If, therefore, these clots had formed, as is supposed, or had commenced, before death, upon the valves, they must have lined the whole of the interior of the vessels at and near their connexion with the heart, and must have completely covered and impeded the action of all the semilunar valves in such a manner, and to such an extent, that it would scarcely have been possible for the circulation of the blood to have been continued at all.

I think that additional observations upon the coagulation of the blood in the dead body, under varying circumstances and after various diseases, must be made before we can agree with the author of the excellent work *On the Coagulation of the Blood*, that either the tubular or the laminated structure of a clot, or the fact of a clot consisting of a fibrinous tube containing red blood in its interior, is conclusive evidence of the coagulation having begun before death. Lamination is a singularly prevalent and remarkable feature in the inorganic, as well

---

[1] Richardson, *On the Coagulation of the Blood*, 407 and 420.

as in the organic world; and the circumstances under which it occurs and the causes which induce it would prove a fertile subject for study and experiment. It is doubtless more commonly observed in those clots which, there is good reason to believe, have formed before death, than in those which have commenced subsequently. It would seem to depend upon the deposition of the fibrine in successive layers; though that is not certain, inasmuch as it may depend upon some peculiarity in the manner of the solidification of the fibrine, the particles becoming disposed in plates and layers, just as we know they have a disposition to be arranged in fibres; and it is no unreasonable supposition that this may, under favourable circumstances, take place after death. With regard to the tubular form of a clot, it is by no means improbable that, in certain peculiar conditions of the blood, the tendency of the fibrine to separate itself and settle upon the walls of the vessels, on the valves, and on other structures, may be manifested after death, in the same way that it often is before death; and may thus lead to peculiarities in the appearance and structure of the clot which render it very difficult, or impossible, to distinguish whether they are *ante* or *post-mortem* formations.

The mode in which the *fibrinous* and the *corpuscular* varieties of the fibrine are combined in the same heart, or even in different parts of the same clot, are difficult of explanation. Thus in a lad, who died with cerebral symptoms after amputation, I found in the right auricle and ventricle a firm white clot which presented, under the microscope, a distinctly fibrous structure, the fibres being clear and delicate, but strong; and in the left ventricle were small reddish clots, containing an unusual quantity of pale nucleated corpuscles. When the two varieties coexist in the same clot, the fibres generally preponderate at the circumference, and the corpuscles nearer the centre: the reverse, however, was found in the clots occupying the heart in the case above related.

I am not aware that the presence of small fibrinous clots dispersed throughout the venous blood, as in the case just related, has been observed by other pathologists, and it is not very easily explained. I recently found them under the following circumstances.

An unhealthy man, who had encountered many hardships, and had long been a sufferer from various complaints, was admitted into Addenbrooke's Hospital on account of a cutaneous affection of peculiar character. It consisted of inflamed and swollen patches of skin, upon some of which the surface became scabbed or blistered, whereas in the others the portion of skin first affected resumed its natural appearance, and the disease spread, ring-like, in the circumference. He had also laryngitis, and was in a feeble state, with difficult breathing and small pulse. He became quickly more prostrate and restless; the difficulty of breathing increased, and after being twelve hours in a dying state, he sank on the sixth day from his admission. The treatment consisted in the administration of small dozes of mercury with Ipecacuanha and Quina and such nutritious diet as he was able to take. On examination twenty-four hours after death, we found interstitial suppuration in the glands and cellular tissue of the loins and pelvis; defined white masses caused, apparently by lymph-deposit, in the kidneys; a swollen and superficially ulcerated state of the mucous membrane of the larynx; a thin layer of recent lymph upon the pericardium and upon many parts of the endocardium; and a granulated state of the inner surface of the right auricle in the neighbourhood of the ventricular opening.

The clots in the right cavities of the heart, and in the trunk and large branches of the pulmonary artery, were large and dark, but presented nothing which attracted attention. They were, however, removed hastily; and any slight peculiarity might have escaped notice. In the left ventricle the greater part of the clot was also of uniform dark colour and consistence. Prolongations of it, however, which branched between the carneæ columnæ at the apex, were rather firmer, and were composed of white and dark portions intermixed; they were only slightly adherent to the lining membrane. I examined the blood in the venæ cavæ, in the iliac, subclavian, axillary and azygos veins, and in the cerebral sinuses. In all these it was very dark; in some parts it was fluid; in others it was in soft black clots; and in the substance of many of the clots were small white or yellowish-white irregularly shaped masses of fibrine. These masses were nearly of the same consistence as the other portions of the clots, and were continuous with them; in some instances they were near the surface, so as to catch the eye directly the clots were drawn out of the vessels; in others they were more deeply imbedded. They presented under the microscope a remarkably distinct fibrillated structure. I did not find any of them in the fluid blood. There were thin continuous coloured clots in the smaller branches of the pulmonary artery, and in some of the other arteries; they presented a natural appearance, and there were none of the pale fibrinous masses which were so common in the veins.

It is, I think, pretty certain that these peculiar fibrinous masses were formed either after, or very shortly before, death, during, or just antecedent to, the setting of the blood, and that they had not moved from the position in which they were first formed. Had it been otherwise, they must have accumulated in the small branches of the pulmonary arteries, and caused obstruction there; whereas those vessels were quite free from them. Moreover, the fibrinous masses shewed no signs of having been wafted along in the blood-current, but looked as if they had, from the first, formed parts of the clots in which they were found. Neither is there any reason to suppose that they were fragments—"emboli"—detached from a clot laid down in any part of the venous system. There was no evidence of existence of any such clot: the fibrinous masses were found in each of the veins above-mentioned; and to have reached these several situations, they must, some of them at least, if they were all derived from the same source, have gone the round of the circulation, and have traversed the pulmonary and systemic capillaries.

Perhaps an explanation of these, and of some other phenomena of a similar kind which are more frequent, may be given in the following manner. It is generally admitted that in certain conditions, in the *living* and in the *dying* body, the fibrine acquires the property of separating from the other constituents of the blood, and of forming clots which are more or less devoid of colour, or which are particoloured in consequence of the red corpuscles being only here and there entangled in the setting fibrine. The theory of the obstruction of the veins and pulmonary arteries given in the preceding pages is based upon this hypothesis. But is it not probable that the same thing takes place *after death*, and with even greater rapidity than during life? The influences which retained the fibrine in solution being withdrawn, any preternatural tendency to separation, or any tendency to separation and coagulation in an irregular manner, which had existed, and perhaps manifested themselves, during life, are likely to be evinced in a more marked manner after death. It seems not only probable, but almost certain, that this must be the case; and if it be so, we must cease to regard irregular intermingling of fibrinous and coloured masses, giving a pied appearance, as the evidence that a clot has been formed before death; we must look for some additional proof, such as adhesions of the clot to the interior of the vessel, or a choking up —a distension—of the vessel, or a corrugation of the clot, as in the case of the burnt girl above narrated, or some other sign of the influence of the blood-current upon it.

In the case of the man, which has just been described, I infer that the colourless portions of the clots were caused by the hasty separation and consolidation of the fibrine, at certain points, after death; and that the fibrinous masses thus irregularly formed were included in the fluid blood, and formed parts of the coagula which were formed in the ordinary way

D

from the blood. Probably, also, in the burnt girl some, possibly the greater part, of the clots were *post-mortem* productions, though, for reasons previously given, it may be presumed that some of them were formed during life.

It may be further assumed, that the tendency to separate coagulation of the fibrine will produce its effects after death in much the same manner, and in the same positions, as during life; and that it will, thus, lead to the formation of fibrinous clots upon and near the valves, upon the interior of the vessels, and between the carneæ columnæ of the heart. In this manner a tubular lining of fibrine may be laid down in the interior of the pulmonary artery after death, and be moulded upon the sigmoid valves while the remainder of the blood in the vessel is fluid. This remaining blood subsequently coagulating would form a soft dark cylindrical clot enclosed in, and continuous with, the fibrinous tube. Still later the contraction of the whole clot, more particularly of the outer fibrinous tube, would draw it away from the sides of the vessel, and leave it free in the interior or nearly so. Thus by a sequel of intelligible *post-mortem* processes we may have produced those tubular fibrinous clots containing red clotted blood in their interior, as well as those fibrinous or particoloured strings between the carneæ columnæ, which have been described by Dr Richardson and others, and which are commonly thought to be dependent upon changes going on during life.

I do not mean to say that such clots are always formed after death, but that they may be so, and that we must be careful ere we admit these and other similar appearances to be evidence that the coagulation of the fibrine has taken place during life.

CAMBRIDGE: PRINTED BY C. J. CLAY, M.A. AT THE UNIVERSITY PRESS.

DESCRIPTION OF PLATE.

FIG. 1. The femoral vein, and Fig. 2, the popliteal vein. There are small coloured fibrinous lumps, also strings and bands and pigmentary stains, and other traces of the former occupation of the vessels by clots. (See page 14.)

FIG. 3. The right pulmonary artery from the same patient, containing a firm fibrinous and mottled clot.

FIG. 4. The left pulmonary artery from the same patient, containing a very firm and closely adherent clot. There are also black stains, continuous with the clot, in the lining membrane. (See page 27.)

FIG. 5. Wrinkled fibrinous and coloured clots at, and near, the junction of the large veins of the neck and arms: *a*, right jugular vein; *b*, left ditto; *c*, right subclavian vein; *d*, left ditto; *e*, innominate vein.

Fig. 1.

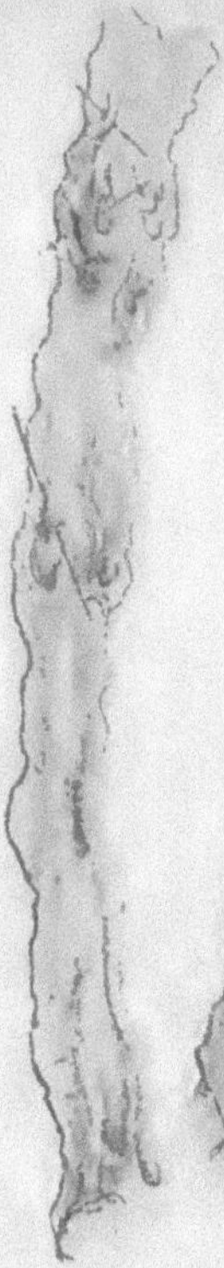

Fig. 2.

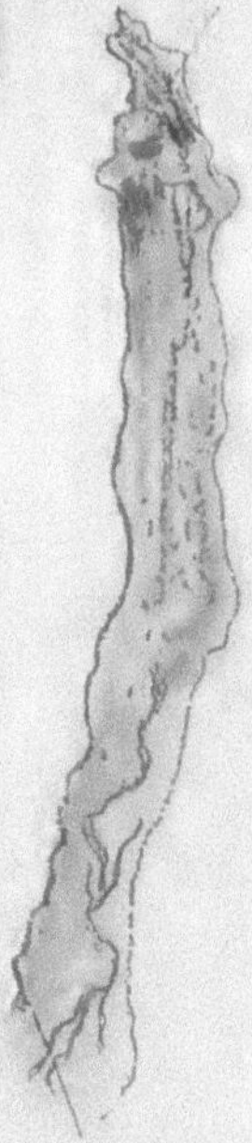

Fig. 3.

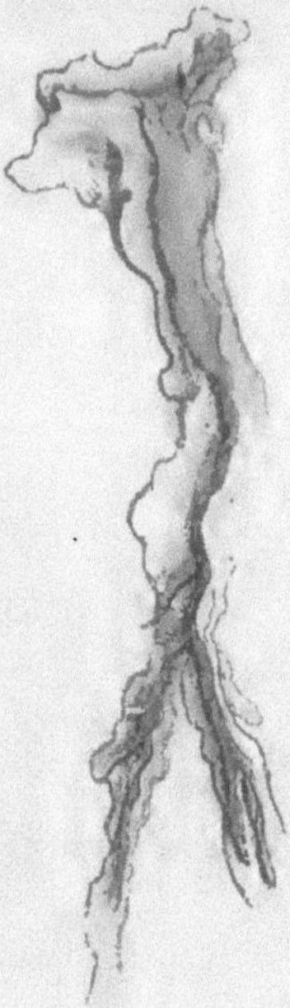

Fig. 4.

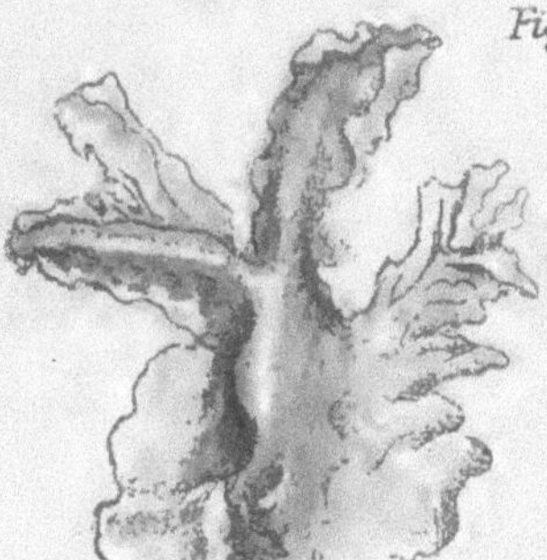

Fig. 5.

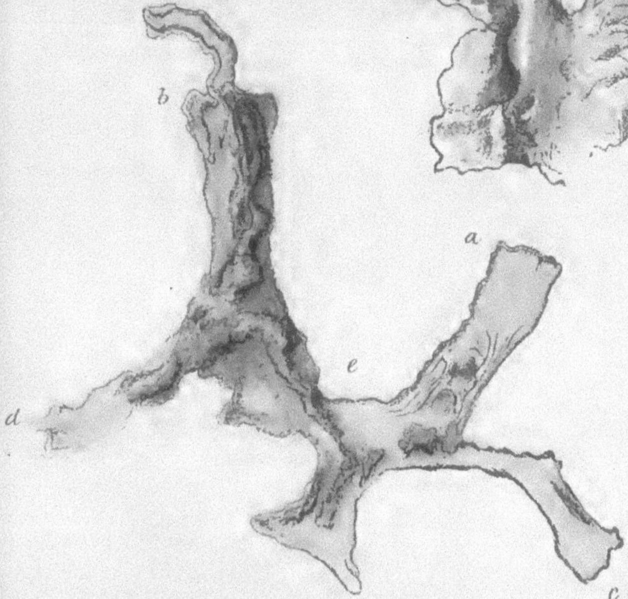

b

a

e

d

f

c